T0380583

THE WIRE.

A futuristic world. Instead of divorce people go back in time to find new partners.

PETER R. SHAND

authorHOUSE

AuthorHouse™ UK
1663 Liberty Drive
Bloomington, IN 47403 USA
www.authorhouse.co.uk
Phone: UK TFN: 0800 0148641 (Toll Free inside the UK)
*   UK Local: (02) 0369 56322 (+44 20 3695 6322 from outside the UK)*

Published by AuthorHouse 03/13/2024

ISBN: 979-8-8230-8681-3 (sc)
ISBN: 979-8-8230-8683-7 (hc)
ISBN: 979-8-8230-8682-0 (e)

Library of Congress Control Number: 2024905619

Print information available on the last page.

THE WIRE – 1

A FUTURISTIC WORLD. INSTEAD OF DIVORCE PEOPLE GO BACK IN TIME TO FIND NEW PARTNERS

CHAPTER ONE

WIRETECH

It works on a traditional cut, copy and paste process. It scans at a microscopic level. Even the smallest detail will trace. eg. Mass, Age, Scars and scratches of you and your belongings. The pasting process is instant and painless.

The Boost Amplifier.

This will ensure that the fade effect thats encountered during photocopying will be impossible with Wire tech. Infact Wire tech travellers are able to become fuller than even before they 1st commuted.

Travel Plus.Com.

Why travel when you can do so much more. Join travel plus today.

Wiretech Make Over.

Remember when plastic surgeons used knifes? They didn't even own a degree in sculpting but we let them mould our faces. This system will allow commuters to receive instant plastic surgery. You will be sent images of several completed make overs, All designed from one of our hand picked freelance Airbrush Beauticians. All you need to do is simply save it or undo it.

Buy clothes, Make up and much more from our Wire tech shops. Our patented software automatically knows which type of products you prefer. This simply by monitoring your past purchases and responses. Simply select my history. Why D.I.Y. When you can get someone to do that for you? This is only available on the safe and store option on Circuit 12.

Accuiel.

Teleportation only takes a minute and that's to anywhere in the World. However our Wiretech travellers may choose to experience one of the various other virtual travel shopper options.

Travel Shopper (e) Market.

You may decide to visit one of our (e) Gym's However these automated services must be pre purchased. This is because your Satnav route must be planned in advance. This can be done via your (e) device online. Simply select the Taxi Wire.

Leroy Brown.

Leroy hasn't been feeling well. He visits his G.P. He G.P. tells him has a new strain of Meningitis. This mean Leroy has 2 weeks to live. The first thing Leroy does is, search and beats up his old high school bully.

The Parade Salon.

Janice Crawford sweeps up after a long day. Her boss aka Miss Veronica McKenzie is smoking her 20th cigarette of the day. Janice ask's "Are you locking up tonight or am I?" Veronica say's "Me" but then she asks if Janice can come in early tomorrow? Veronica has got a date tonight and she wants to sleep in. Janice smiles and says "ok." She puts her coat on and leaves the Salon. She walks around town for an hours worth of window shopping then home to her runt pussy cat called Barrell. First she wants a cheese Burger.

Mitchell Meets Janice.

All the staff call Mitchell sir or Mr Armstrong. He travels back in time. It's a busy Friday night in the city. Mitchell has just brought a cheese burger from Kerry's mobile booth. Janice is standing behind him. She over hears him showing off about having parents who never ever smacked him. She punches him in the arm. He turns and say's "What's that for?" Janice replies with a smile. She say's "You must of done loads of things wrong when you where a child and got away with it. That's for all those times I got a smack."

Proposition.

Mitchell Frank Armstrong all but falls in love at first sight. He wastes no time. He simply straight out tells Janice Amy Crawford the truth. He tells her "My Name is Mitchell. I'm a multi billionaire from the year 3005."

"I paid for the right to be able to travel back in time. This inorder to adjust certain aspects of my life. This popular but very expensive phenomenon is known as a Re -Take. I invented the concept and being wealthy means I am fortunate to practically have unlimited access to such ventures. This is my 7th sorry my 8th attempt at finding the love of my life. I'm offering you a chance at my heart. For love. I do not have children and I don't want any." He pauses, smiles and awaits a response.

Obviously the 22 year old Janice does'nt belive what she has just heard. However Mitchell has a simple plan to change that. He shows her a News Paper. It's has tomorrows date. He shows her page 4. Boy killed in traffic accident. Mitchell walks a short distance to an exact location. He proves he's not lying by saving the young boys life. He called the boy over and offers him £10. He tells the boy "First you got to tell me a joke. Any joke."

"Why Did The Chicken Crosses The Road?

Mitchell interupts and say's "No chicken and road jokes. Not from you kid." He gives the boy £10 any way and sends him on his way. Janice Witness the news paper article change. The boy was suppose to get hit by a bus but the number 17 C went past without incident. The boy would of died probably chasing that ball he has in his hand.

Unconfident.

At this current moment in time the young Mitchell is 25 years old and single. The old Mitchell is 35 years old and Married. He meets his first glamour model wife to be next week. Janice has no seductive moves what so ever. How does an average girl steal a rich man from a glamour model? "I cant compete" She say's after Mitchel shows her a picture. Mitchell calms her down. He say's "Firstly I only meet my Wife to be on Monday tonight." You've got to be there at the party where I meet her. All you got to do is pull me. This is important. I end up marrying that Woman." Janice isn't even sure she can get him even if she puts it on the plate.

Make Over - Wiretech Face Mask.

Mitchell say's "Your right you don't stand a chance against her. However this is also my invention." Old Mitchell can change his appreance using the Wiretech face mask.

Travel Shopper Style

This will give you a 360 degree holographic images of yourself, Wearing any clothes from any designer. This p.o.v means you will also see what other people will see when you wear what you wear." Mitchell say's "Why simply shop when you can shop on the Wire? He smiles but she does'nt get the joke. He shows her how easy plastic surgery is done via Wiretech. He gives her a ridiculously large noise and mouth. Janice say's she want plastic surgery.

New Posh House.

After the make over Mitchell buys her a house. Janice is lost for words. "I haven't even pulled you yet." Mitchell say's "I've got faith in you." He shows her a new Porse and a Bentley. She points at herself. Mitchell nods. Whether you succeed or not.

Work - Monday.

Janice does'nt want to go to work. She's self conscious but Old Mitchell insist she tests her new look out. Obviously her boss Veronica is surprised to see the new Janice. Veronica ask's questions after questions after questions. Then say's "Your fired. Who did this? I want them working for me?" Janice say's "I did this." Veronica say's your re hired."

5:00 pm.

In walks the old Mitchell Armstrong. He introduces himself to the gob smacked and jealous Veronica. He also hands her a bunch of flowers. He asks if Janice is ready? She say's "Yes." Mitchell's Cheauffer opens the Limo door for Janice. They drive away leaving Veronica in shook.

Introduction.

Their at the party. Old Mitchell reminds Janice why it's important for her to pull him tonight. He points out his younger self and his glamour model Girlfriend. Young Mitchell invents his first working teleporter in 3 days. Old Mitchell say's "Young me has hit a brick wall in this project that's why he's out tonight. He thinks he needs to let his hair down." He say's "The girl i'm with in 3 day's becomes my muse. This moment burns into my mind and heart" He say's. "I've re - taken this night 7 times and I always fall in love with the girl that i'm with when I complete the first teleportation of a living object.

Club Network.

Young Mitchell is with lots of pretty Women. He's already well off and well known for being brilliant. His confidence is unmissable. The Women are not shy about being interested in him. From nowhere Janice shout out "Prenumital Agreement." She catches young Mitchell attention. He smiles at her because 1 or 2 of the Women actually walk away from him, shaking there heads.

Question. What Does Young Mitchell Armstrong Like In Women?

Young Mitchell Dances with Janice. She even buys him a few drinks. She shows him her Porce key. It's almost too easy. However she suddenly starts to feel guilty. She goes to the ladies room. Old Mitchells worried.

Guilt.

Janice returns. Old Mitchell ask's "What's up?" She asks "Why not go for an ex who knew you before you where famous? Old Mitchell say's "I have tried it and it works for a while then it fades out." Janice sighs and say's "Maybe you should keep working on your current wife. Mitchell say's she's cheated on me....several times. I've cheated on her too. It's over. I was only interested in her beauty and her body anyway. That's why i'm here. Janice say's give it another go?

Gina Walker. Wife Number 7.

That's Mitchell Armstrong's current Wife. He travelled into the past and returns with Gina. He reappears exactly where he left. He Introduces her to Janice. Gina wants a re take too. It's another chance at Love. Unfortunately another girl has pulled Young Mitchell. It happen while he was in the future getting his wife.

Leroy Brown 2.

He spends his live savings on scratch cards. However he doesn't win. So he robs a bank. He uses a taxi as a get away car. He's no longer nervous around Women. He's so confident he pulls a pretty girl but not just any girl, He pulls a glamour model.

Fashion Week Party.

They've spent every day with each other. Young Mitchell turns up with his current girl Friend. Her names Brittany Knocks. Janice arrives with Old Mitchell as her Date. Young Mitchell recognises her. She tries to make Young Mitchell jealous. They kiss and even ballroom dance in front of him but it does'nt work.

Saturday Night In.

Somehow Janice must be there when young Mitchell achives the first successful teleportation of a living organism. Old Mitchell can tell Janice is Frustrated. He ask's "So your a Beautician? Why did you choose that profession?" "I enjoy it" responds Janice. He smiles and say's "That's important. I enjoy my work too. It's almost as important as wages isn't it?" Janice comments that she would very much like to experience more aspects of the Wire. Especially make overs.

Mitchell tells Janice that the Wire salons only employ people who have degrees in Art. They must have at least 2 years experience. He thanks her out the blue. She say's "No thank you, I'm flattered. Your rich, hansom and you chose me. Not even just for sex either but for Marriage. You know i'm taking you for all I can get, If this does'nt work out don't you?" Mitchell stops smiling.

Mitchell tells her he has passed on her details to his law Firm. "You'll have rights now. No matter what. Not yet but soon. All you need to do is say you worked for me and for how long. I pay well. You'll get a couple of mill out of me. That's not quite taking me to the cleaners when your as rich as I am. She asks "How much are you worth if you do'nt mind me asking?" He say's "At least a Trillionaire. I was being modest before."

He pours her another glass of wine. Janice Smiles but tries to hide it. She looks around the room nervously. He notices the Awkward silence kick in. Janice puts down her glass and takes his glass off him and places it on the table. She say's "It's a brand new sofa and carpet." He kisses her and that night they make love.

The Morning After. Pillow Talk.

Janice ask's "What happens to you if I get the young you to fall in love with me?" Mitchell say's "Delete." That person is me now. Remember if he died now I would die too." "Ante you worried that someone will come back in time and kill the young you" asks Janice? "Who would want to kill me ask's old Mitchell? And remember I invented time travel. Coming back in time to kill the young me would be dangerous. All of a sudden old Mitchell suddenly Disappears right before Janice's eyes. Someone knocks her front door. They're from the future. They brake into Janice's house. She escapes via the back garden. She locks the door.

Betrayed.

Old Mitchell has been teleported back to the future against his will. His lawyer Dennis Fisher is pointing a gun at him. Several members of the board are present too. "How could you" Ask's Mitchell? "It's not just me it's the entire board and several of our investors" responds Dennis. Your monopolising time and transport. Dennis the lawyer say's "They were going to kill the old you but I suggested they kidnapped the young you instead. Once we do that we'll own you. You are the companies prize asset afterall.

Stake out.

Janice catches a taxi. It's 9:00 o'clock. Janice is spying on young Mitchell. He's home. She can't see anything. A few hours go by before anything happens. His new girl friend aka Brittany teleports outside young Mitchell's house. Janice tries to phone old Mitchell but again she get's no reply.

The Day Everything Changes.

Young Mitchell completes his first successful teleportation test. He and Brittney kiss each other in celebration. It's 9:00 pm, Janice knocks Mitchell's front door, He answers. Janice tell's him that he's in danger. His girl friend can teleport. "I just saw her. How would I know of Teleportation?" Young Mitchell recognises Janice. He thinks to himself. He has a bad feeling. He still say's "I don't believe you." She say's "You know something must be wrong." Young Mitchell say's "I don't trust either one of you." He drags Janice inside the house. He asks himself what should I do?

Brittany is in the other room. Mitchell tells her "I've got a bottle of champagne in the fridge will you get it for me? First she ask's who was that at the door?" He say's "Just a neighbour complaining about the noise again." Brittany walks to the kitchen. Young Mitchell stands in the centre of the teleportation device. It's known as the spotlight area. He tells Janice "I'm teleporting away from this house, Your staying here." The teleporter counts down. Janice say's "No way am I staying here." She stands next to him and holds his waste.

Brittany has the bottle of champagne. She see's Janice with Young Mitchell. She pulls a gun out of her handbag. She's been ordered not to kill young Mitchell. She aims the gun at Janice but it's too late. Young Mitchell and Janice teleport away just in time. Brittany phones Dennis he tell's her to try switching off the teleporter. It's a transmitter teleporter. Young Mitchell has gone to the receiver teleporter. Dennis expects young Mitchell and Janice to return to the transmitter teleporter, If the signal is switched off. Brittany does as she's told. She prepares her gun and waits but young Mitchell and Janice do not return. Dennis say's next time shoot him in the knee cap.

Young Mitchell and Janice should of transported to young Mitchells other house in country. Dennis's army raid that home and discover that Mitchell and Janice never arrived. Their assumed dead. Dennis has to appollogise to the board. He say's "We still have the old Mitchell. The young him was no threat to our plans."

Cross Connection.

Somehow young Mitchell and Janice have teleport into the future by mistake. Their in old Mitchell's Mansion storage room. Janice ask's "How did we get in the future?" She suggests it's because she has old Mitchell's number. Young Mitchell's impressed. He say's "No it's probably simply a cross connection. I had no idea my teleporter could also be a time machine too."

Fail safe.

Young Mitchell marvels as he looks outside. He looks at his worn out prototype aka his failsafe. He talks to it. "You could tell the difference could'nt you." It still works and it's still plugged in. "Your the first person other than me who's seen this device. I've never told anybody about this and I never would of just incase someone came after me." He has a key hanging on the door. Janice say's "Lets just go to the Police." She ask's "How do they get to a Police station?

24. 09. 3005.

Young Mitchell types in Police. The computer ask's "Do you want the dectector Unit?" He types more information. All incidents are reported to the relevant services first, Then the emergency services investigate the report. If a crime has been committed time is reversed and it's simply undone via the detector unit. If a crime isn't reported it will go unchecked. Young Mitchell selects the internet. He asks a question.

Question: Who Invented Time Travel?

Profile of Old Mitchell Armstrong appears. He is the official inventor of teleportation and the man commonly associated as the inventor of time travel. Click select to learn more about costs? Janice tells young Mitchell who she is. "Your married but your getting divorced." "How bad is the divorce ask's young Mitchell? Is she trying to kill me?" Janice say's I don't think she's involved in this." "From what I saw it's an amicable divorce." "Maybe she's in danger too ask's Mitchell?"

Young Mitchell searches the net for the nearest Police station. It's 10 miles away. "Let's walk" say's Janice. But young Mitchell say's no. He turns on the tv. It reports the arrest of a murder. The Woman he murdered say's "I was shocked when I was told that he murdered me. If it wasn't for the wire I'd be dead now. Old Mitchell has an Indian maid. Young Mitchell introduces himself to her. He explains his dilemma. She tell's him that his wife moved out a few months ago. She takes them to a Police station.

The Police Station.

The Police station isn't very big and it only has a few members of staff. Their clearly not use to visitors. Young Mitchell explains all. They give him a DNA test which he passes. He tells the Police officers that with no real Police force, Ruling the World will be easy.

Young Mitchell and a Police Officer search through time. There is suppose to be only 1 single timeline. This is young Mitchell's timeline. If anyone goes back in time to change the past that's suppose to effect the future. Law and order is easier to manage with this principle. A Police officer agrees but he tells young Mitchell and Janice. "You can't stay here."

A Police officer is ordered to go to the local Wire office. A teleporter device costs no more than a fridge so even the Police station has one. The Police officer teleports to the Wire office. He takes young Mitchell and Janice with him. He ask's a member of staff a few questions. The staff give him their full support. He looks around and is about to leave but all of sudden a member of staff who's been held against their will, Shouts out for help.

Unfortately the officer is shot. He drops his gun. Young Mitchell picks it up and shoots 2 or 3 of the Wire staff. Everyone thinks the Policeman is dead but he's still alive. He manages to call for back up. Other Police officers raid the Wire office and it is'nt long before they kill or arrest all of the Wire staff.

30 minutes after the shoot out a Police officer informs young Mitchell that various Wire staff have used force to take controll of the Wire offices in London, Washington, Paris, Berlin, Moscow and Sydney.

The Wire - Main Headquaters - London.

A member of staff confirms the things that they're going to change. Change 1 to 17 are all varified and cross checked. They start the countdown - 10 minutes and counting. Old Mitchell ask's Dennis "What are you up to?" Dennis explains his vision of a new future.

Monopoly.

Dennis say's "I told you I would not kill you but I didn't say I wouldn't kill the young you." The young you will simply be found then murdered."

Mitchell smiles and say's "You haven't found him.......me." Dennis say's "Once we kill the young you, We'll share the wealth.... equally. The terrorist computer programmers turn off their teleporters. The Police must drive there.

It isn't long before the army make their way into the Wire main head quarters. The Terrorist are completely outgunned. All the Police officers are busy so young Mitchell and Janice try to sneak away from the Police visitors room and into the Teleporter office.

Obviously the Prime Minister has been informed about the terrorist threat. He has also been told that young Mitchell has travelled into the future from the past. The P.M wants to find out if he will still be the P.M, When time is changed. Young Mitchell uses the laptop that the Policeman left behind. He uses it to hack into the main Wire headquarters. He and Janice teleport straight into the Wire office, even though their Teleporter was switched off. He Teleports into the main headquarters call center. The shocked Dennis ask's young Mitchell "How the hell did you end up here ....in the future?" Young Mitchell say's "I honestly don't know." Old Mitchell say's hello to Janice she smiles at him. Dennis flees for his life.

The members of the board run away. Young Mitchell uses the laptop. He tries to stop the count down, While old Mitchell chases Dennis. He resives a call from Kevin Holt aka the head of the board. Dennis tells them he couldn't predict that young Mitchell would travel into the future. He tells them all they can do is try to hold out until they can rewrite the past. That will happen in 2 minutes. Old Mitchell catches and beats Dennis up. Dennis say's "The countdown has begun, Your too late." Old Mitchell asks Dennis "Why would you do this to me?" Dennis shouts out "Money and Women aka the things you got." Old Mitchell say's "If you wanted a rise I would of given you one. You've earnt it. I Apologise but obviously your still sacked."

Young Mitchell is struggling to prevent the boards re take. Time will restart at the exact point when young Mitchell had his first successful teleportation. Old Mitchell stands behind him and starts telling him what to do. Unfortunately young Mitchell has already tried everything he's suggesting. Janice say's "Just turn it off." Young Mitchell ask's old Mitchell "Will that work?" Old Mitchell say's "There are a hundred computers in this office and this is a World wide effort.......no."

Young Mitchell ask's "How long would it take for you to go back in time? "Old Mitchell say's "10 seconds........Top." He and the Police use the teleporter to find the exact moment when Dennis gave his takeover presentation to the board. Time is rewritten. Dennis and the board are all arrested. All the innocent people who died are resurrected. As with all crimes the information of this case is released to the press.

Mitchell Changes The Law.

It's been 3 weeks. Leroy visits his G.P. The G.P appologises. Apparently Doctor Boldric was looking at the wrong file when he gave Leroy his diagnosis. Leroy attacks the Doctor. The Doctor presses his panic button. Leroy is arrested.

Before young Mitchell and Janice travel back in time young Mitchell goes down on one knee. He ask's Janice "Will you marry me?" She say's "No" she say's she's not in love with young Mitchell. Old Mitchell ask's her to marry him. She kisses old Mitchell on the lips and say's yes.

The News.

Nobody else will be allowed to Re - take life simply for matter of love and romance.

The End

THE WIRE – 2

SYNOPSIS

Billionaire Mitchell Armstrong's memory is wiped and he is sent to an alternate dimension.

CHAPTER ONE

It's the year 3010 Millennium parties are being planned all over the World.

The New Law.

Prime Minister Janice ....has just announced the parent law. If a Women has evidence that her husband has Fathered a child with another Woman, She will be granted the right to have him sent to one of the various human slaughter houses. Women can also kill Men without the use of a slaughter house. e.g If he is violent against her. Men do not hold this privilege. This is mainly due to the fact that he will never be allowed to kill an unborn child, even if it was Fathered during an affair. A Women can't kill a Mother to be too but she can kill the child's Father.

How Did This Law Come About?

The TV expert say's "This is a simple case of powerful Men who became addicted to the underground female dominatrix culture. Now Women can actually get away with murder. Yet meanwhile in the upper class society the Men still dominate.

25 year old Mitchell Armstrong has been arrested. Last night he saved a Man from being taken to one of the cities slaughter houses. He didn't only beat up a Police officer, He almost bit his noise off. Mitchell is questioned in court. The Judge ask's "Why did you bite him?" Mitchell say's "I like the taste of pork." Some laugh until the Judge slams his hammer and barks out commands of "order order order." Mitchell almost responded by saying

"I'll have a large pizza.....everything on it." Mitchell is sentanced to two hours community service. He has no intention of doing a minute.

The Dark Stranger.

It's the early evening and Mitchell orders another Beer which is teleported to his table.

Valentines Day.

Mitchell and his new friends burn down 4 or 5 wedding dress shops that night. Infact Men all over the World are going on a wedding dress shop burning spree. 3 hours later and the gang go back to one of the 24 hour pubs. Leroy buys a large bottle of rum even though Mitchell's been drinking Beer. Everyone knows you should'nt mix your drinks. Soon as Mitchell gets drunk Leroy starts to tell him a strange secret.

The Secret World.

Leroy tell's Mitchell that there are facts that your yet to be taught. The reality of alternate dimensions for example. Leroy knows that Mitchell is basically drunk. He tell's Mitchell that there are Governments that experiment their sick new laws on other weaker dimensions. Mitchell is too drunk to process the information but he still ask's Leroy "Why keep it a secret?" Leroy say's "Because if your not with them your against them. That's why they teach you such things as the slave trade. They want your faith in society to waste away. They laugh at you and say Women can now kill Men. What kind of wife would do that to her husband? The issue is that they can legally kill you now if they want to. So the question is do you think the laws protecting you?

The Next Morning.

Mitchell wakes up in Leroy's big posh Mansion house. Toast has already been made. Leroy ask's Mitchell "Do you remember what I told you last night?" Mitchell has a flash back. He say's "I didn't pay any attention last night but I remember." Leroy says "Its time you learnt the story don't you think?

Leroy say's "This is the first World. It's the dimension where I was born. Years ago our Goverment made contact with a new Dimension. The 2 Worlds created a new law. The winner would gain financial rewards. The question was which World will be able to uphold that law the best. It was a peace contest. Which World could be the most peaceful dimension. 911 and the holy war happened in this World. The neighbouring World remained peaceful.

This was about forgiveness. Punishment still meant failure. However soon it became too competitve. Not long after first contact our relationship started to turn violent, A war was inevitable. It was a war we lost. The reflection rulers took over the Governments of this World and forced it into a regression.

Before the war, People from both Worlds where allowed to travel from one World to the other. That could have been the single big mistake that ruined this World. The inhabitants of our World aka the 1ˢᵗ World went to the refection World to better it while the inhabitants of the reflection World or the new dimension came here to ruin this World.

Hell.

Leroy's master, Eric enters the room. He interupts Leroy. He say's "That's how you get the murder laws of this World. Now you know. You where born and raised in hell" Leroy tries to stop his Master but he continues talking. He say's "Your northing more than a living reflection. You and everyone from this dimension. Everyone you hold deer amounts to northing more than a shadow. Mitchell laughs but it has a hint of a anger. He softly say's "Leave me alone."

Leroy's Master continues his story of alternate dimensions. "There's more to this story but I wo'nt tell you yet. It'll be the kick of adrenaline that you'll need to finish the Parent law off once and for all." Leroy tell's Mitchell that if the Police ever ask why did you riot? Never say because of alternate dimensional corruption. They'll kill you or put you in a mad house for sure

Arrested Again.

The Police raid Leroy's Master's mansion at 4 am. Mitchell is taken to the Police station for questioning. He tell's the Policeman "I only met those blokes for the 1st time last night. We had a couple of drinks in the pub and before we knew it we where burning down wedding dress shops. We ruined a few wedding cakes to. Is that a wrong thing to do?" The Police suspect that Mitchell knows about dimensional travel. There's a little spark in his eye. He's detained awaiting deportation.

Mitchell makes an enermy in jail. A 45 year old man called Barry Crawley. Fortunately things never manage to get out of hand.

Scramble.

Mitchell is found guilty of being a terrorist. His memory is Scramble and he's banished to the dirtiest dimension of all. This World appears to be in the beginning of the old millennium. Mitchell is homeless, He's uncoordinated, He talks to himself, He's an alcoholic, He finds it difficult to even communicate clearly.

Meanwhile.

The unified dimension alliance movement aka the U.D.A M complain about Mitchell's treatment but their ignored.

The 1st World - Arrested Development.

London's landmark building's such as Big Ben and the Houses of Parliament still stand. The debate is whether London's architectural history has slowed down the rest of London's development. This World is clearly in a state of depression, The population has an even divide of races, The common man is considered as poor.

It's a mild Saturday evening. A charity worker helps Mitchell get his life back on track. It's 1 year on since he was deported. He has a home and girl friend. She see's him thinking to himself. She ask's him what's wrong? He says "I do'nt know, I just know something isn't right. I can't put my finger on it." Monica tell's him "You need to stop smoking weed. That's what you need to do." He laughs and look's up to the sky. He notices a cloud that has a similar shape to the Eiffel Tower. 7 day's later there's a terror attack in Paris and the Eiffel tower is destroyed. Does Mitchell have a 6th sence?

2 weeks later he notices another strange cloud. This one look's like a car. For some reason he put's faith in the strange cloud. Instead of driving he decides to catch a train. He even puts a lot of money on a horse called full throttle. He looses but later on that afternoon he's told that his car was stolen and it was involved in an accident with a lorry, Killing the driver.

Mitchell starts to watch the clouds through a telescope, Then he start's recording the clouds with a camcorder. He decides to tell his girl friend, Monica about his theory. He tell's her about his strange ability to see future events by watching clouds. Monica tell's him he need's professional help. Mitchell is sectioned. Monica tells Mitchell "I know you saw the Eiffel tower in the clouds, Then the terrorists destroyed it. I know, I understand but the clouds are not talking to you."

One or two of the hospital patients claim to have 6th sence abilities too. Jack Cole can talk to dead people, Robert Sunderland has extreme O.C.D which makes him addicted to smelling other people body waste. He's also an Arsonist. He insists that he knows why he is mentally ill.

Robert Sunderlands Theory.

A nameless Scientist theorised that positive thoughts can be transmitted from person to person. This was attempted however a hidden enermy of mankind decided to use it as an opportunity to turn cannibalistic. They studied the brain specifically to figure out certain vital zones. E.g Laugher, Sexural Stimulation and Intelligence. Each region produced a slightly different chemical. These chemicals are now considered as a unclassified drug which are now being milked out of the human mind for human cannibals who are from an alternate dimension. The hidden issue was the fact that obviously certain slave owners in the past where Homosexual. We can assume female slaves where raped so we must assume some males where too.

Mitchell does'nt sleep very well that night. The next morning he notices another strange cloud. This one is shaped in the form of a tall building. He calls his named nurse. He tells her about the cloud.

Sky T.V.

Mitchell watches sky news all day instead of clouds. But northing major happens. He starts to believe he needs help. He even starts to take his medication. He notices another strange cloud but he ignores it. A week later and Monica tell's him she's pregnant. She discovered the news a week ago. She didn't tell him because she was worried the news would frustrate him.

Mitchell is unsure about his ability. A movie convinces him that he might be able to see the future afterall but he now realises that he can mistranslate the message. He explains this new information but he can tell the power hungry named nurse isn't exactly listening. The Doctor ask's "At what point will you start to accept that your mentally ill?" Mitchell say's "I already think i'm mentally ill."

The Fire And Miscarriage.

Mitchell is released from the hospital. He and Monika row every other night. Mitchell becomes violently aggressive. He drinks all day and all night. Eventually Monika ends their relationship.

Soup Kitchen.

Mitchell is homeless again. It's 9:00 am, He goes to a soup kitchen until it closes. That night a stranger offers to share a bottle of whiskey with Mitchell. The stranger is Leroy and his owner Eric aka Father Stephens.

The Pub Brawl.

He takes Mitchell to an members only pub. The Landlord takes Father Stephens money but refuses to serve Leroy. Leroy beats them all up on his own. He tells Mitchell to stand up too. "I'm going to help you, let's go to my house. You can have a shower and stay the night. I'll even make you breakfast tomorrow morning.

Once there Leroy starts to talk to Mitchell. He mentions the 2nd part of his alternate dimension story. A few decades ago the 1st unified dimensions law was passed and it was an overwhelming success. Other laws where passed too there after."

He teaches Mitchell about the murder laws.

"These laws have been in effect for a long time. Men just except it now. Human Men have been turned into broken horses and there are other ridiculous laws on the way. Do you want to hear some?" Mitchell shrugged his shoulders then he responds. "My heads going to explode so do you mind."

The Alphabet Game.

"There are Politian's who have a invested interest in corrupting stats and evidence of the alphabet game. That's how we get legal slavery. There is also evidence that suggest some law's have'nt been past because they'll produce a utopian society in the first World aka your World."

Reverse Prohibition - Using Heavy Machinery.

The people decide to ban all Politian's from drinking alcohol and taking certain types of drugs.

Modern Politiions knew about the reverse prohibition act. Obviously the goverment has a time machine. They used it to inform the US Pentagon about the reverse prohibition. The intel was delivered to the president in 16 January 1920. They created the prohibition law as retaliation.

Memory Retracer - Flashbacks.

Leroy opens his laptop. He visits the Wire website. He opens the memory retracer. Mitchell is still a little drunk but he's told to steer at the screen. "The less you blink the more you will remember." Mitchell steers at the strange patterns. He slowly regains his full esteem.

The Alphabet.

The next morning, Mitchell wakes up in Leroy's big posh mansion house. Toast is already made. Leroy asks Mitchell "Do you remember what i told u last night? Mitchell has flash backs. He says I didn't pay any attention last night but I remember.

Leroy's friend steers at Mitchell. Leroy say's it's time you learnt the whole story, don't you think? Mitchell does'nt answer. Leroy tell's him 1st of all there is another world. Years ago our Goverment made contact with that other dimension. Long ago this alternate dimension invented a device that created our dimension. Together we, us and them started a simple contest called the alphabet. The two worlds would create a brand new law. The winner would gain huge financial rewards if it's citizens broke less laws. It was a peace contest. The winner would be who ever could be the most peaceful dimension.

Imagine a northing to loose game where both societies simply played to see who could be the kindest. It's the total opposite to what it is now. It was never meant to be an eye 4 an eye competition. The new dimension citizens where known as reflections here. Our rulers took over the Governments of the other world and forced it into regression. The alphabet competition was all a trick. We acted as if we where better than those barbaric reflections because we where winning. In reality the bet was all a con. It was to late by the time we figured them out. Peace what peace. There is no peace.

Before the war the people from both worlds where allowed to travel from one dimension to the other. That was the big mistake that ruined this world. The inhabitants of the 1st world went to the reflection dimension to better it while the inhabitants of the reflection dimension came here to ruin this world.

In there dimension the alphabet peace contest is common knowledge. They've covered it up in this world now

This is hell. Some say that your the descendants of the evil souls from their world. Many holly manuscripts explain who and what they are. One thing's for certain is that the dimension is evil beyond all recognition. That became obvious once they won the war.

Hell

The reflectors were'nt reflectors. They was not identical to us in apperance. Yet somehow they manage to kill the man in the mirror but it's also clear that this dimension is changing. That's why you don't know about the peace contest. Your rulers made laws to keep the peace but there evil to the core so they do it in the only way they can. In the evil way.

because your from hell. I'm not sure if your the descendants of the evil souls from our world or not. Many holy manuscripts explain who and what you are. 1 things for certain is that your evil and beyond all recognition. That became obvious once your won the war. Murder laws in so many worlds.

some reflectors were identical to us in appreance not all. Somehow you manage to kill the Man in the mirror. But it's also clear that the reflection dimension is changing. That's you don't know about the peace contest. It wants to be what the 1st World was. it wants to swoop places. Your leaders act like you think were in heaven or something. Your rulers made laws to keep the peace but there's evil to the core so they do it in the only way they can. In the evil way.

That's how you get the murder law. Now you know. This is why you are the way you are. It's because you where born and raised in hell? Leroy tries to stop his Master. But he continues talking. He say's your northing more than a living reflection. You and everyone from your dimension, everyone you hold deer amounts 2 northing more than an evil shadow. Mitchell laughs with a hint of a snarls. He softly says leave me alone.

Mitchell Armstrong.

Mitchell say's "I know who I am. We must try to close this dimension. If we close the open program it wo'nt exists. All we have to worry about is whether I can hack it and close it before they come here. He spends all night but fails to hack into the Wire. Father Stephens tell's Leroy "The retracer didn't work. This isn't the Mitchell Armstrong I knew."

The Reflections.

Leroy tell's Mitchell do you remember I told you that people do not have identical reflections in terms of apprence. Some people believe that if your from this World your most likely to be a good person if you have an identical reflection. Leroy say's "Tomorrow i'll introduce you to your identical reflection twin."

The Burning Cross.

Father Stephens say's their here for Leroy. He has to leave. Unfortunately he is shot as soon as he opens the back door. Mitchell see's a burning cross in the garden. A lynch mob walk towards the house. Fortunately the Police arrive in time to save them. Mitchell, Leroy and Father Stephens are arrested. Their taken to the maximum security prison.

Corruption.

Mitchell has met Leroy in two different dimensions. Leroy explains his back story. It started ten years ago, Political Corruption is widespread. The wealthy want to maintain their dominance. They invent the crown law. Criminals can now share their punishment with their friends and family. That's not only for minor penalties. A volunteer can do time in prison for you. This means the criminal will legally remain free. "That's who I am."

The Crown. Reality Series.

Leroy asks Mitchell "Do you watch it?" Mitchell says "Not really." First they tell the story behind the crime then TV viewers get the opportunity to donate aka volunteer to do time in jail for the contestants. Mitchell say's "I know of it but I don't watch it." That weeks episode involved Frank August. He's a wife beater. He has been sentenced to 3 months in jail for his crime. However he has proof that he had been viciously attacked by his wife in the past. He didn't get anyone offering to help him. He did the full term. "I was contestant 2 say's Leroy. He presses fast forward on his phone.

Trial 2. Gangland.

Leroy Masson had the potential to be the next Daddy of the Chilling gang. But he was told he had to earn his stripes before that could ever happen. Stripes translates as he has to kill someone from a rival gang. His mark is Rachel Isle. Aka the best looking girl that the rival gang has. She's not even dating the Daddy of the Hangers gang. Yet Leroy Masson put 5 bullets in her in a drive by shooting.

Thanks to an anonymous tip off he was arrested by Police a week later. It becomes clear the 50 years old current Daddy of the Chilling Crew aka Marlon Welsh has tricked Leroy. Marlon then tells his Crew not to volunteer anytime for Leroy. However the other members of the Crew turn on Marlon. One evening he's kidnapped. He actually tried saying that he was only testing the other members loyalty for Leroy aka the no.2. They ask "Did we pass?" Marlon say's "Yes you pasted."

The new no.1 aka Leroy is out on bail, He kills Marlon in cold blood. Leroy's 10 year sentence is shared with the rest of the members of the gang. He remained the new Daddy while still being in jail. Leroy say's "I'm a Murderer. When I got out Father Stephens took me under his wing. He showed me that turf warfare is a waste of time. The war is against the law makers.

Steel Bars.

It's the biggest payday most boxers will ever get. It's aired live from prison. It's a great way to ensure the prisoners can continue supporting there families financially while in jail. Priority's have a way of changing with or without the consent of your the best laid plans. The Warden tell's Mitchell he has to fight. His

opponent is called Kieran Davenport.

Lil Tim.

He tells Mitchell he is donating his time. He's doing time for a Man who tried to steel some bread to feed his children. "The shop keeper had a gun. He fired at the shop lifter but missed, He shot another costumer. He only wanted to feed his four kids. I couldn't let him do time, So I offered to do the whole term. I don't have any children myself. I'm glad I could do something with my life that I can be proud of." Mitchell lets Lil Tim be his number 2.

A few days before the fight and Mitchell get's a call from the Police. A 3 year old Girl has been found murdered in the woods by the one stop shopping complex. It's his child. The Police do not have any clues as to who did it.

Funeral.

Mitchell is allowed to leave jail to attend the funeral. The law states that Leroy, Mitchell and Father Stephens have the right to be put on the reality program called the crown. Leroy tell's Mitchell he guarantees they'll get released soon.

Westminster.

Member of Parliament, Luke Crown argues with the other P.M's. He insists the crown court reality programme is a disgrace and it should be abolished. The Prime Minister deny's the charge. He throws stats that support the claim that the crown is a deterrent to crime. Luke Crown say's it allows people to get away with murder. The speaker is outraged. "Order! Order! Order!" Luke Crown says "Order? I'll have a cheese burger and large fries. He's find 12k for that remark.

Prime New Debate.

Should they cancel the crown television programme? The PM insists they should not. Luke crown also points out that he has evidence that billionaire Alan Strute has been making large financial payment to the Goverment. The PM insists funding has always been apart of politics. He deny's ever receiving a personal payment from any of the billionaire's companies.

Arrest.

The Son of billionaire Alan Strute is Arrested and Released from custody. He's suspected of being a child killer. He killed Mitchell's Daughter. However he'll definately escape life in prison because his billionaire Father will simply pay someone to do his time for him. Mass Poverty means there will be alot of volunteers begging to do the billionaires Son's time. It's hard to financially support a family in this kind of society. This maybe the best opportunity some Fathers will ever get to secure their families future.

Free - Magazine For Men...... And Women.

The models in this mag often escape serious crimes. Certain Fans are only to pleased to volunteer to keep certain Women out of prison. Lot's of Women do pornographic material with avid fan's knowing it means the fan had volunteered to do time for them. The son of Alan Strute openly admits to murdering Mitchells and Monika's daughter during an television interview.

Murder Outside Of Club Free.

Monika kills Alan Stute's Son in cold blood. 3 bullets to the chest and 1 to the head. She's wrestled to the ground by his body guards and arrested, She's quickly found guilty on all charges. The billionaire calls for the death sentence and he get's his wish. It will take place in a weeks time. Northing can reverse a death penalty decision. This means if someone does Monika time they will resive the death penalty in her place.

Monika phones Mitchell. He ask's "What about your new boyfriend what's he doing to help? Monika say's "We split up ages ago. The relationship was never very strong." Monika say's "He does'nt even answer his phone in case I ask him to do the time for me." She then refuse's to let Mitchell do her time. She has no remorse for what she did, none what's so ever.

The Green Mile.

This is just a dummy run. Monika walks the mile and sits in the hot seat. Each mock step is carried out. She's on the way back to her cell when she's introduced to a Man called Ronald Stable. He own's a magazine called the Catch. Monika knows of it.

The Catch.

The Men who run this magazine are professional donators. However these hunks only donate if it guaranteed to lead to them making a porn movie with the convicted Women and only the pretty Women. They want a movie with the Girls for every month they spend in jail. Once agreed the deal is lawfully enforced to ensure Women perform to their agreed written contracts. If she changes her mind she get's sent back in Jail.

Ronald Stable offers Monika a lifetime contract. He shows her his last movie. The porn star beat up an old school bully to death. She only got sentenced to 5 years. "I called her a few weeks back and asked her if she's now warmed to the idea of making porn for a living. Do you know what she said?" "Yes" say's Monika, "She said yes."

Ron suggest Monika allows him to have a word with the Prime Minister. They have an understanding with each other. "Your sentence will be reduced but then you'll be mine or should I say you'll be free. Free to work for the Catch." Monika say's "I'm listening." Ron say's....... "Forever." He ask's "Are you in or are you out?" She say's "I've go to talk to my ex." Ron say's "He'll be some piece of work if he rather you died. "Mitchell has been granted a Conjugal visit. He immediatly volunteers to face the electric chair but again Monika refuses to except is donation.

The Last Meal.

Ronald visit's just after Monika's last meal. He has a new contract. He now wants her to work for free. Aka no charge. Monika's done for so he can take liberties. She's got no bargaining chips left. She say's "Jesus your not messing around are you? Is there anything else you want. A double d boob job maybe?" Ron points at the contract and say's "That's already been written in. Your going to be huge." He arrigantly stands up and say's "I send the Men your way and you deal with it or you go back on death row." He ask's "Lovey dovey or fast n furious?" Monkia picks up the pen and say's "Lovey dovey." She asks Ron to send good looking Men. He say's "I'll try my best, I Promise." Monika signs the contract and blows a bubble with her chewing gum.

Fame.

The decision not to allow anyone to take her place has made Monika very famous. It's 8 o'clock, The prison guards enters her cell. He tells her the law is under review and no one else will be executed in her place. The main influence to the overruled decision happened in West Minister. The leader of the opposition, Luke Crown volunteered to take Monika's a place. Infact 35 Labour Politicians also volunteered to be executed in Monika's place. Monika was'nt told. The law had to be changed. The Prime Minister contacts Ronald Stable and informs him that his contract agreement with Monika is now void. Monika is released.

Ronald Stable once said "Love is a kin to addiction and that's simular to the attention gained from fame. That's what keeps girls in porn." He's offering Monika a new paid XXX contract. She refuses. He tell's her "Your the girl that got away." It's 10 pm, Monika arrives home. It's almost like Monika and Mitchell are back together, However she tell's Mitchell to leave once she catches him taking Heroin.

A Few Day's Later.

Leroy see's Mitchell taking the anti psychotic medication, Theocileen. Leroy calls Father Stephens. He ask's Mitchell "What's it for?" Mitchell say's "Delusional thoughts." Father Stephens ask's "Do you hear voices?" Mitchell say's "No." Father Stephens explains that some cases of mental health problems might come from the fact that crocked Police are trying to prevent certain people from accessing certain parts of their brain. Supressing is known to happen in both dimensions.

Father Stephens ask's Mitchell "Have you ever witnessed a murder but you failed to identify the suspect?" Mitchell say's "No." Father Stephens tell's Leroy "This is why the Police released you from prison. You was still on your meds. They knew your not the real you." Leroy visit's the same website as before. Another yet slightly different procedure is carried out. A few moments later and Mitchell say's "I remember who I am. I invented a time and inter dimensional travel device. I invented the Wire."

Father Stephens tell's Mitchell that who ever did this to you also planned that your new mind be fragile. Eventually you would end up in front of a shrink and end up on that type of medication. Mitchell tell's Leroy that they need to go to the reflection World. Someone has altered time and I need to find my Wife."

The Reflection World.

Mitchell builds a teleporter. It only takes him half an hour. Father Stephens say's "This is the real Mitchell Armstrong." He and Father Stephens go back to the reflection World. However two strangers have somehow managed to hitch a ride with them. One of the strangers explains his story. "I was a well known player. This means I and other Men travelled back in time to sleep with Women before they get famous. It's an underground competition. There is millions to be won if your the one who manages to pull a specific star." He went back in time but fell in love with the mark. "She married me even after I told her the truth about who I was and why I was there. However the organisers kidnapped me and sent me to one the gold mines." Mitchell ask's "What gold mines?" The stranger say's "The goverment created a multitude of alternate universes for one specific reason. A gold rush. Gold from an endless supply of alternate Earth's. There is so many of us that I managed to escaped during a riot. It'll be a day or so before they notice that i'm gone."

The Other Man Tells His Story.

"The Police blatently came to my house and told me they where going to bid for my Wife. She pretty no lie. I sold everything I had and I was still out bided. I could of brought two girl's with that money. Anyway I tried everything to get my Wife back. One day I snapped. I broke into her new house and killed her new husband. Right in front of her. She did'nt even know me. They asked me how did I remember the past timeline?" I said "It happened after a car crash. My life flashed before my very eyes. Suddenly I saw who I was at this age but in another timeline. I remember loosing my Wife. That's why I attacked him." It was him who bought my Wife. They sent me on the mines too. The stranger suddenly realised that he's talking to Mitchell aka the Man who built the Wire. Mitchell appollogise and promise to undo what went wrong. Father Stephen tell's the stranger's Mitchell is the priority. If we can help him we will all be safe.

That Afternoon.

Mitchell tell's Father Stephens "Someone has used my invention, Went back in time and created this reality. They rewrote our lives to that of a World who's inhabitants lost an inter dimensional war called the alphabet. Father Stephens say's "bingo."

The Omega Bet.

Mitchell finds out where Janice lives. He Teleports to the Janice Williams mansion. Why isn't she called Janice Armstrong any more? A Man called Carl Williams greets Mitchell. He ask's "Do you know who I am?" Mitchell say's "No". Carl say's "I'm Janice's Husband. I married her in the dimension where you married her. But I married her first." Mitchell say's "You murdered her." Carl say's "I should of killed you." Mitchell say's "Why didn't you?" Carl say's "I can actually remember how much I hate Janice. Mitchell say's "You killed her for over cooking the Christmas Turkey. Carl say's "i'm going to divorce her, After I kill you. What did you think about the Alphabet?" Mitchell say's "There's no way that was your idea." Carl say's "Your right. It was the board."

The Contingency. The Omega And Delta Bet.

Carl say's "The reflectors aimed to imprison mankind, Within the Bible. They used the very commandments as chains. Meanwhile the reflectors will do the exact opposite as and when it suits them. Hence they might of called the competition the alphabet but it isn't the first attempt to manipulate mankind that way. The alphabet is the promise to obey the law. However there's a omegabet too. The omegabet bet was the promise to obey God. The first World has stopped the alphabet competition but it still holds on to the principle of it.

"This Bible is and has always been a con. The concept of following this Bibles commandments was as I said the deltabet. Jesus promised that all human sins would be forgiven. This allowed Mankind to be free. This freedom was suppose to be a reflectors principle. Only they where suppose to have the freedom to be evil without consequence.

"We tried and succeeded in installing the concept that crime meant punishment not forgiveness. That separate concept was favourable to our own ends. Jesus died on the cross for mankind's sins. His sacrifice is a message. The story of Moses means thy shall not kill. The Bible can also be interrupted to mean do not follow Gods orders without question. Unfortunately there is a time to steal and a time to kill. But as I said we chained Mankind with the laws of Man and God.

Mitchell Stands Over Carl.

Janice enters the office and she shoots Mitchell before he get's a chance to explain. The Police arrive they inform Carl that they have managed to track the venue of Mitchell's teleporter.

Mitchell had set up the teleporter. Carl tell's the Police to re-hack Mitchells mind. He's too impatient to wait. He starts typing on his computer. Unfortunately it's too late Mitchell's sign is sent. A moment later and the entire World wakes up to reality in other Worlds before Carl altered it. Janice remembers who she use to be. She remembers Carl and a timeline she lived before Mitchell changed it. Janice tell's the Police to arrest Carl. His plan of taking Mitchells place fails. The Police have evidence that he and many others have altered time and pocessed innocent life's.

Hospital.

The operation to take the bullet out of Mitchell is successful. Janice stands over him as he opens his eyes. She kisses him as soon as he wakes.

A Week Or So Later.

Father Linton Stephens was a professional football and father. The 44 year old often wished that he could go back in time to redo his footballing career. He met Carl Williams and was offered the opportunity to go back in time and he took it. However one day he bursts into tears after he realises that he misses his Wife and Family. He then desperately waited and sort out a way to get back to his old life but that was impossible.

Linton Stephens became Farther Stephens. He still knows that he was once friends and saved the richest man in the World. In a reality that no longer exists. Mitchell tell's Janice about Monika and his daughter. This time he's the one who's unwilling to delete the other World. However the law is the law. There must only be one timeline. He has no choice. The reflection World is deleted.

The End.

THE WIRE – 3

A SERIES OF NEW TECHNOLOGY MALFUNCTIONS CREATING A EXTREME SHIFTS IN WEATHER

News.

CHAPTER ONE

POLAR/SOLAR ENERGY - 3005

The Wire has created hostile weather patterns. The World is in a new ice age one minute and extreme global warming the next. Mitchell Armstrong has memory loss issues however he has still managed to master the art of polar energy.

As well as oxygen and fruit, Plants where successfully re-designed to produce electric. Machines where now genuine power plants. This technology has been condemned by environmentalists. The new ice age had a dramatic dominoe effect with all other living organisms which included Humans.

Threat - The Earth's Axis.

Scientists suggest an old ice age may have caused the Earths axis. However this new threat was dismissed. A solar power ban is require at several times of the year. This is similar to the hoes pipe bands of yester year.

The Alcamist.

Year - 3015.

Mitchell is trying to become an alcamist. The theory is that alternate dimensions will not be nessusary if alchemy becomes reality. He has been recently qouted as saying that "We must live with our scars. Our children are more important than we are. The future will be built for them."

This recent statement does'nt deflect the fact that the Worlds nations are complaining about the fact that Mitchell is responsible for the recent ice age. The price of Mitchell's companies stock crashes.

Stuart Price - Inventor.

Scientist Stuart Price invites Mitchell to his London Restaurant. Stuart has been trained in several martial arts. He can endure pain and freezing temperatures by simple Human hybination. He can fall asleep at anytime within a second or 2 and remain so for day's on end. He put's his hand over a burning flame and rolls his eyes to the back of his head.

Code name. Loadstone.

Stuart Price gives a presentation. He shows two animals. "We can explain how these magnificent creatures prove the evolution theory. The question I asked is what do I have to extract from animal b inorder to turn it back into animal a?" He uses a device which instantly turns animal a into animal b then he turns animal b back into animal a.

He explains that he made his breakthrough once he considered that evolution is a seperate living organism It's not based on desire, need, circumstance or enviroment. It's intelligent. Once you understand what temperature does to water, you can boil it or make ice. Once you understand evolution you can make other animals as intelligent as Humans.

Apes are simply the only species to maximize their potential. However every animal still has the ability to do it. After the demonstration is over a reporter ask's "Will Humans be allowed to evolve or unevolve into various other animal species? Stuart responds "We will see."

Shift In Power.

Mitchell watches the Morning news montage. The young Stuart Price has taken over Mitchell Armstrong's position as the years highest earner in the World.

Richard Traine - Politician.

He is a influential member of Parliament to those who have supported Mitchell. He also warned the public about alternate dimensions. Even he can no longer protect Mitchell but he still tries to prevent Stuart Price's political intentions. Stuart's Family is also now Mitchell's new neighbours. Mitchell's still invites Stuart Price's Family for dinner and he excepts.

Obesity.

Mitchell's Son is fat. Infact a large population of Humans have become over weight. Mitchell's Teleportation device (The Wire) has been named as the primary cause.

Saturday.

Matthew Pallet is Janice's and Mitchell's caterer. Mitchell is surprised when Matthew resigns his post a day before the big dinner. He say's he has a new job opportunity. It's either get a new chef or the Family cook for themselves. They get a new chef. The next chef is blind, She's called Gale. She insists her sence of taste is amplified because she is blind.

Dinner and Camping.

The Dinner went as hoped. Both Families politely eat around a large table. The hassle of the past few months lends Mitchell to insist that his Family go on a camping holiday. They went that very Sunday. Mitchell is comfortable in the great outdoors. He knows alot about animals wildlife and plants.

The New Winter.

The temperature is 30 degrees. Janice only has hay fever but Mitchell mocks her by calling it Aids. "You get every cold that goes around." She laughs and tries to kiss him but he moves away. He tell's her "Your not kissing me with your Aids mouth." She say's "We had sex last night, If i've got Aids you've got it now." He say's "If you give me Aids, I wo'nt be able to sleep with anyone else. That's why you did it." She laughs.

Code Name: The Crossover.

Mitchell's Family was only away for a weekend. However the following Monday Morning he goes to work and discovers that Stuart Price is lobbying to get the death row principle implemented into law in this timeline. He is getting alot of support. However Mitchell makes it clear that he will oppose him.

Richard Traine.

Richard Traine insists that Mitchell is holding back the World. Why have World with a 100 different Countries when we can have a 100 different Worlds. Each country get's 1 World. No one can stop the majority from getting what they want. It'll mean war if you even try.

Cyril Is Ill.

It's a disease that lives in the sand. It has mutated and become life threating and widespread. Many tried wearing masks but it didn't work. Several Doctors refuse to look after his child once they know it's his Son. Janice complains to the Police. She asks "What type of Doctor refuses to look after someone?" The Policeman say's "They can refuse to see patients." Mitchell responds, He ask's "Shouldn't they have to explain why? I'm sure you can understand that as a Black Male i'm flabbergasted that I can get persecuted for simply asking if a person was being racist towards me or not? It shouldn't take an intelligent person to notice how ironic that is. Afterall there has been many cases of racism even in the modern day. E.g Murders, G.B.H. Most ironic is Racist Language.

"I suggest the refusal to support me confirmed that there maybe a more sinister reason for the two cancellations. I understand that a patient must be patient. I also believe a Doctor is suppose to want to help a patient. They said I called them racist. However I was simply trying to inform them that I was beginning to question whether they wanted to help me. They confirmed my concerns by officially refusing to help me. If it happened in a Dentist it would remind me of Sweeny Todd.

Assault.

This is a type of assault but they didn't punch my Son in the face. They just deliberately dragged out the operation. Reminds me of Hannibal Lector. Doctors who Murder their patients. It happens but this is new to me. This way they didn't even need to beat him up.

London.

Janice and Mitchell find a Doctor who is willing to help their Son, Cyril. However they must travel all the way to London and the Wire still isn't working properly.

The Sands Of Time.

The temperature is 40 degrees. An entire Family dies from teleportation via the Wire. The cause is blamed on sand in the systems. At the moment telephones still work. By the end of that night, The temperature was minus 10 degrees.

The Traffic Jams.

The weather becomes so much warmer that it's predicted that this years winter will be hotter than last years summer. Every road everywhere has a traffic jam. Most cars don't work. Janice and Cyril are in London, Mitchell is home alone. His Neighbour, Nicola Sunderland has always had a crush on him. She makes a pass at Mitchell but he rejects her. She ask's "Why have'nt you gone to London?" He say's "It's too far. I get travel sickness, That's why I invented a teleportation device. She does'nt except his excuse. She still thinks she has a chance with him.

Life Alone.

One of Mitchell's ex wife's come to visit. She makes a pass at him but he turns her down too.

News - Temperature Shift.

Weather conditions can dramatically change from desert conditions to polar conditions in a instant. Last nights Lightning Storm killed 8 people.

Rule.

Stuart Price's loadstone device malfunctions. It alters his DNA, He randomly turns into various different animals. From a Bee into a Lion. He concentrates and manages to gain suitability of his mind. He starts to be able to transform his DNA into any animal he wants to, at will. He can even evolve into an improved Human. Unfortunately by the end of that night the loadstone device begins to absorb the essence of Humanity out of him completely, He turns wild. He can not turn into a simple Human anymore.

Stuarts insane mind insists that Human's are his enemy. They have ruined the Earth. His appreance changes into half man half bull. He waits until all his staff arrive at work then he turns them into a new animal predator. His monsters are Human but instead of Ape they are designed to evolved from other various animals. His managers are granted the DNA of all the Worlds most dangerous, Poisioness plants. He tells his monster army that he is their king. He calls himself, Rule. He tell's them to hunt the Human race and eat. A News flash warns the general public of the attack. By the morning most streets have developed it's own Neighbourhood watch system.

Mitchell's Quest.

Monsters attack day and night however their still only animals. The Goverment allows guns to be distributed free of charge. It's 7pm, A worried Janice phones Mitchell. She gets through on her 4th attempt. Mitchell convinces her that he is safe. She has no choice but to tell him that Cyril needs his DNA to survive. The temperature in London is 35 degrees while in Birmingham it's minus 30 degrees.

The wire isn't working so he Mitchell has no choice, He's going to have to walk to London. He pack's a bag and prepares for his journey. He leaves that night. The streets are almost empty. That's not only because of the monsters. It's mainly because of the weather machine malfunction. There is hardly any shops left open.

Henry And His Family.

They live in a caravan that has been stranded in a traffic jam for months. Their one of the lucky Families. He offers Mitchell a bed for the night, Mitchell accepts.

12 am.

Mitchell and Henry are tipsy of moonshine. They talk about race and racism. Henry say's "Not many black persons have travelled to the north or south pole." Mitchell say's that's not because white Men are better athletes. It's probably because it's white as far as the eye's can see, There's northing but white there. What type of black person want's to see that." Henry laughs then he say's "White people like the sun too you know. Me personally, I get too tied in the summer. Mitchell say's "global warming."

Mitchell Learns How To Ride A Bike - Montage.

Henry is about to teach his 4 year old Daughter anyway. Mitchell keep's a video journal. The internet connection is so slow that it takes a day before Janice watches it. Cyril's health is getting worse, He's almost past the point of no return.

The Sandstorm.

Mitchell Can Ride a bike. Mitchell buy's Henry's Daughter a bike. After a while he realises that he can cut time of his journey by using a short cut. However he'll have to travel through Cleet Woods. He decides against it. He rides his bike on until he's hit by a sandstorm. Snowstorm are as common as rain was. He waits it out in his tent.

Instead of roads Mitchell follows the railways. The trains don't work either. Several families live in the carriages. One night Mitchell is robbed by a Polish gang. They take everything. Including his bike and tent.

The Trainer - Paul.

Phone services finally completely fail. Mitchell meet's an Author called Paul Lingway. Pauls famous for training dangerous pets to be obedient. He thinks he can train Rule's monsters. He works with Dogs because Man has been able to controll evolution in them for years. That's why there is so many different breeds.

Racism.

Mitchell and Paul are talking about monsters. Paul say's "The colour of your Dog does'nt matter when your measuring it's intelligent. Superiority happens but it's mainly due to the breed of Dog. It's the same in the Human race too.

Paul tell's the story of Noah ark. "After the great flood God promised mankind that he would never flood the Earth ever again. Today the World has become a desert. Water is already becoming scarce. This is another warning from God. Love your neighbour."

Destination Arrival.

Mitchell finally make's it to the Hospital. Janice is ill again but this time she say's "It's not hay fever. This time it's a common cold that's going around." Mitchells missed her so much that he does'nt care, He passionately kisses her lips. She say's "I can't believe you still kissed me, You never do that when i'm ill" He ask's "Have you been with another Man?" She say's "No way," Then she ask's "Have you?" He say's "No but Nicola fancies me." Janice ask's "Nicola Sunderland? Does she really?" Janice clearly start's to reminisce about circumstances where Nicola had opportunities to pull or flirt with Mitchell.

That Night.

Mitchell is buying something from the vending machine. All of a sudden Rule's monsters attack the Hospital. Mitchell and a few others manage to hide in the church area. After half an hour the coast becomes clear. Mitchell rushes to his Son's room. Amazingly both him and Janice are still alive. Nurse Lewis tell's Mitchell that the monsters only killed a few people. They took dead bodies from the morgue. They did not attack the patients who have contagious diseases....Like Cyril. Janice sneezes and blows her nose. Mitchell say's "Not even monsters want to catch your Aids."

Wire Tech Enemies.

TV Chef, Richard Pallet joins forces with Stuart Price aka Rule. Rule's monsters had him surrounded. Rule offered Richard a job as his Chef. Richard now makes a menu of new foods. Foods with Human as the main ingredient.

Black Gold - The Hospital.

Rule has created a mobile teleporter. He is funded by Mitchell's board. Mitchell ask's Rule why? Rule say's "This is not about the gold rush that you stopped. They do not want gold or precious stones anymore, Now they want........ oil. Unlike Gold and Diamonds, Oil won't loose it's value. But that's not the point either. They insist that you have persisted in turning yourself into the dictator of time/Dimensional travel and it will lead to the demise in their standing. Rule reminds Mitchell of the 1 World 1 dimension law. He ask's Mitchell a question. He ask's "How can your law be overruled? Mitchell answers, He say's "Only if the World faces an extinction level event." Rule say's the Wire malfunction was a plan to ruin your reputation and create an extinction level event.

Democracy.

Surprisingly Janice agree's with Stuart. Mitchell say's "I do not agree with democracy. Some decisions are my decision. Not everything can be put to a vote. I do'nt agree with majority rules." Stuart offers to reverse Wiretech malfunctions. He laughs and say's "We simply need to turn off a device in my lab." They teleport to Pricetech headquaters but the security guard recognises Mitchell. He refuses them access. The security guard is half Human, Half Pig. Stuart use's his mobile teleporter. It's simply an app on his phone. He absorbs the security guard into his phone. Stuart sends him to the Birmingham office. Mitchell, Janice and Stuart make their way to the main Lab. Stuart turns off his weather machine and his machine that caused Mitchell's teleporters to malfunction.

Stuart vs Mitchell.

Stuart say's "I can make as many versions of myself as I want." He simply presses a button on his mobile teleporter and he creates an identical clone. Mitchell wants Stuart's technology. Stuart say's the older they are, The more intelligent they are. This is my first clone. I used the loadstone device to turn him into an advanced/evolved Human. He's not made using the DNA of a Elephant. Even though they are apparently the most intelligent animal other than Humans. I removed his Ape DNA with Human DNA.

Unfortunately Stuarts own clones turn on him. They kill him. Stuart rolls his eyes to the back of his head. The monsters are following the orders of the first clone aka Clarke. He picks up Stuart's phone. He teleports the other versions of Stuart into his phone. Mitchell takes the chance to escape.

Clarke has become more compassionate than Stuart. He questions Stuarts wrong doings. He searches for Mitchell and Janice. He appologises. He has reversed both of the deliberate sabotages to Wiretech. He even offers to help Cyril, "I'm your last hope, What have you got to loose." Janice can tell this Clarke has changed. They all teleport back to the Hospital. Clarke successfully creates a medicine that will cure Cyril.

Then It Rained.

Clarke say's Mother Nature survived the recent drama and this is how. There are microscopic organisms that mastered the art of flight before Humans and even Birds. They did it by leaning how to capitalise on the evaporation process. They used it the way Humans use air balloons and the way plants use wind to pollenate. These micro organisms hitched a ride into the clouds. There is always an understanding within animals. Some microscopic organisms hitched a ride but only until the next rains., Others have learnt how to stay in the sky for months on end. They can travel from country to country that way."

The weather has stabilised. Before they knew it the Earth had turned back to normal. Apart from the fact that England has actually grown by 5%. Many Scientist now wonder whether it would be better to search for new bacterial life in clouds rather than the surface of distant Planets.

No more monsters - Clarke Price.

Clarke say's "First we will replace the Ape DNA from each Pricetech members and monsters, And then they will be replaced with Human DNA. "I do not believe in God. We will create a new species of Humans in my image. We will follow the footsteps of God but we and more importantly I am not God." Clarke say's "Goodbye" to Mitchell. He pulls a funny face before he is teleported. Cyril smiles.

Mitchell Armstrong.

The ban on alternate dimensions still holds. No matter how extreme evil get's, It's our responsibility to fix it. We will not be allowed to throw lifes, Civilisations and Planets away. There still is only 1 way that the law can be overruled. That is if this World faces an extinction level event. Richard stands. by Mitchell's side.

The Establishment Threaten To Murder Janice And Mitchell' Son. They call Mitchell the Devil. He laughs, "The Devil? Mitchell say's I'm not the Devil but if you harm my family i'm going to kill you all. I tried to help you. The Devil whether it be a he or it be a she will be far worse than me.

The End.

THE WIRE – 4

BILLIONAIRE MITCHELL ARMSTRONG IS DRAFTED INTO THE POLICE FORCE INORDER TO FIND TIME TRAVELING SERIAL KILLERS

CHAPTER ONE

--------◆◆◆--------

TIME REFRACTION

Fire Alarm.

The Students and Teachers of Bolington School calmly walk down several flights of stairs. Cyril's friend, David say's "Were all going to burn to death because our school is too cheap to buy teleportation devices for each building." Cyril's other friend Manjit say's "Your here, Your Dad should pay for it, it's not as if he can't afford it. Hello!!! Riches Man In The World."

Next Lesson - 3 Hours Later.

Mr Blame say's "Teleportation improved household health. It revolutionised the toilet. Waste material does'nt reach the surface of a toilet any more. It's teleported directly to the various waste management plants. Mr Blame Asks "What else was revolutionised by the invention of teleportation? Mitchell's son Cyril raises his hand. He say's "The hoover. At first the dust was sucked directly into bags, But my Dad improved it further until the dust was teleported to a specific plant and turned into recycled bio energy."

Teleboard.

Instead of writing, Students and Teachers can print thoughts directly onto an electric tablet simply by pinching the side buttons on the teleboard.

The Neighbours.

Cyril is 6 years old and he's still fat, He's shy too. Michelle Nunez goes to the same School and lives on the same street as him. He watches her through his bedroom window. She's helping 80 year old Misses Fox with her shopping. Misses Fox is scared of teleportation. Michelle also takes Misses Fox's Dog, Pep for walks in the local park.

Virus.

Mitchell is browsing the internet. He resives a new email. It's addressed to him but he has no idea who it's from. It's from a company called Pocket. He opens it without knowing it's a virus.

The Next Morning.

Mitchells has a photograph of his ex girl friend. Beth Humphreys. She died before Mitchell's penultimate remarriage. They met in Jamica. He still has a photo of the night they first meet. He looks at it but somehow the photo has changed. Beth isn't in it. He tell's Janice and then Police but nobody belives him. He studies the wire technology. Is it malfunctioning?

The Next Day.

Unfortunately several people have got the strange computer virus too. Time has been altered as if the photos where taken a few seconds sooner or later. It's not a matter of life or death but it still must be addressed.

Time Refraction.

The time refraction virus has altered the circuit of time. This means many old still photographs can now appear out of shot or out of focus. The Goverment will allow British citizens to travel back in time to retake photographs of loved ones and special occasions. The Goverment warns citizens of the risk of altering time. Wire travel is ATOL protected.

Mitchell complains that time travellers will be able to travel into their younger bodies/selves. He wasn't allowed to when he use to retake his marriages. All Mitchell's past wedding photos have slowly been ruined.

One or two of his old photos are now taken a day after they were originally taken. So his wedding photos are of complete strangers. However he and Janice decides not to time travel. Their old relationships are in the past.

Presentation - The (e)Musket.

Mitchell searches the internet. Giles Remington aka the Prime Ministers consultant presents his range of Ray Guns. Ill Mental health is on the verge of being solved. This signal diminish anger signals to the brain. It works with any animal wild or domesticated. Successful trails confirm this invention deletes anger. This means the British Empire can declare war on the World and they won't want to fight back. This is World war 3. Mitchell downloads the blue prints for the (e)Musket.

Time Rush - The Summer Of Love.

We can go back in time to retake old photographs. So everybody goes wild!!!. Everyone is going on the holiday they had when they were younger. Their taking pictures of loved ones who are now dead. Before traveling everyone is shot with the (e)Musket. Every street is buzzing but in time however slowly but surely life returns to normal.

News.

Last night an angry Man called Mark Pennel was sedated using the (e) Musket. He discovered his older brother had been in a relationship with Mark's 15 year old daughter. He insists the Police had no right to sedate him. He insists anger if not violence is the correct emotion and attitude to have when in this situation. The Police spokesman simply reply's "The (e) Musket is designed to solve disturbances of the peace. We must act first investigate later.

Sync.

People talk out of sync. A person talks but the words are up to 10 seconds late. It doesn't happen every time someone speecks.

Test 45 - Dow Jones.

The Establishment aka Mitchell's board, Aim to create a World where votes can be bought and sold. Imagine votes available on the stock market. In this new World a persons vote is worth more if they're wealthy or talented. A Doctor maybe worth a 100 votes while a homeless Man will only be worth 1 vote. This new ft - index covers status and standing not only merchandise. It's already technically happening.

They will become Presidents and Prime Ministers and it will all be base on their stock market value aka their popularity. This is related but not completely connected to money. Some people are old money however a self made Millionaire may be considered as superior to someone who's old money. Because they had to work harder to become Millionaires. Once this concept is perfected elections and the traditional vote will be obsolete.

The Anchor.

As you know an anchor must be triggered once you time travel into the past. It's what allows us to monitor time travel. This anchor erases the possibility of creating alternate universes. This new, Foreign anchor means the Establishment want to delete our timeline. The last 5 years that we know will not exist. So far we are able to block their anchor's signal. We have stopped the Establishment from setting a new timeline. We predict we have two more days before their anchor stops our anchor.

English General Election.

First you visit www.vote.com. Type in your full name. Your census status/ details will appear on the screen. It will tell you how much your vote is worth. If your selling your vote, It will also tell you the buyers value.

The (e) Musket - b.

We are living in a World of peace. However Richard Traine wins the General election. He is now the Prime Minister of England. Giles Remington comes second. That night Giles changes his (e) Musket a into

(e) Musket - b, It's the opposite of sedation. It makes people have a short fuse. The electric laser colour is red. The original (e) Musket laser colour is blue.

The Collision Risk 60%.

The new Prime Minister, Richard Traine tells Mitchell "We need you to hack into the Establishment's anchor. Richard asks "What are they up to? "Mitchell agrees to facilitate the defence of the present. However it takes longer than it should. His memory lost makes his job much harder.

The army does'nt need telepods any more. They are sent to a remote area to reduce the chances of collision or accidents. It's the year 2029 Mitchell hasn't been born yet. Why does the Establishment want to change the year 2029?

Mitchell eventually works it out. There isn't anything in the year 2029 that they want change. The Establishment knew they wouldn't be allowed to time travel, They created the refraction virus. This would encourage the General public to call for loose laws regarding time travel. Mitchell travels back home.

The (e)Musket vs The (e)Musket - b.

He travels into telepod 2. He gets a physical check up, Then he's given the all clear to leave. It's 10 oclock and Janice and both hear gunshots. A news flash comes on TV. The reporter say's the streets are full of Families Friends and strangers who are arguing with each other, Road rage over minor incidents. Violence is everywhere. Large numbers of the Police fire (e)muskets to maintain controll. Richard Traine is clearly responsible for this. Some have joined forces with Richard. The two sides fire at each other. The reds and the blues. The Establishment fire red (e) Musket laser beams at the Army while the Army fire blue (e)Musket laser beams at them.

By the end of the night. The chaos is happening all over the World. The Establishment use Richard's (e) Musket - b to create an extinction level event.

Evacuation.

The World is in chaos. 1 thousand of the most accomplished British residents are taken to a tropical island. 200 other Women where taken simply due to their physical appearance. The Royal family are left behind.

Mitchell puts his recyclables into a bin. A member of the reestablishment is sat in his Van. He shoots Mitchell in the back with the (e)Musket - b. The curtains are drawn however Mitchell looks through his living room window. Mitchell goes on his teleboard. He types in my backs hurting me. Then types Hate.......Kill.......Kill......Kill, He starts a argument with Janice. He calls her every name under the Sun. He even starts to get violent. He regains controll of himself. He runs away from Janice while he's still got some controll of his sences.

Janice phones the Police. Unfortunately the Police are busy. Mitchell has joined a mob who are attacking the Police Station. Mitchell can't concentrate. Hundreds of Men, Women and Children attack the Police station. They're over run. Mitchell is about to hit a Police officer with a brick but another Police officer shoots Mitchell with the (e) Musket. Mitchell drops the brick.

Holiday - Private Plane - One Week later.

Mitchell, Janice and Cyril go to Jamaica. On the first day, Janice talks to the local VooDoo Doctor. He tells her she will have another child soon. Later on that day, The Voodoo Doctor's Son is involved in a bank robbery. He takes Mitchell as an hostage. Jamaica only have traditional fire arms. The Police raid the bank. The Voodoo Doctor's Son is killed.

Pep And Kronos.

Michelle asks if she can take Misses Fox's dog for walks? The 80 year old widow say's "Yes". Michelle and Cyril start to walk their dogs together.

The Next Door Neighbour.

Tina Field tell's Janice that she has decide to visit the past. She had a Girls only holiday 20 years ago and the photographs are all ruined. Janice confirms her and Mitchell are not time traveling. Tina say's "You go on your own, It's not as if he hasn't had his share of other wife's." She appollogise as soon as she say's what she said. Janice forgives her. "It's true." Say's Janice but that's what makes his decision more romantic. The old him would of gone.

Top Ten Most Realistic Scenarios Where Ugly Men Pull Sexy Women.

1. She's pretty and she's suppose to wear glasses but she does'nt. Hence you only pulled her because she did'nt go to Spec Savers.
2. She's a Adult Performer. One normal day your spotted by a desperate agent on the verge of being sacked. It was your lucky day.
3. You pull the hottest girl from your neighbourhood. She obviously know's you like her but for some unknown reason she always thought you were cute.
4. Her boy friend prefers open relationships. He let's her cheat but only with Men he isn't threatened by.
5. She's pretty but everyone else apart from you had already got her into bed.... a long time ago, Now it's your turn.
6. The Man thief – She's better looking than her best friend, who you have started to date. She's been sleeping/Steeling the odd boyfriends from her best friend for years.
7. She's a drug addict prostitute - You got there in a moment of weakness - Plus you recently came into alot of money, You point blank asked her for a no holds barred one night stand - Shame on you.
8. B.F.L - Aka a shoulder to cry on. She's depressed and your a good shoulder to cry on. You could of totally taken advantage of her but you didn't. A week/months or so after she needed emotional and maybe even financial support you got her. You didn't try it on that night because you was in a relationship at the time. Good for you.

The Call.

Janice is cooking a late meal. She notices a stranger walk into her back garden. They steer at each other. He runs away. Janice gets her gun from the safe in her and Mitchell's bedroom. The living room curtains are drawn. Janice looks outside. She notices a Van which is parked on the street. It was also there the night Mitchell turned into a Zombie. A hacker is in the Van. He uploads a virus into his security system. He tell's his colleague "This means the Armstrong Family can't use their teleporter device to escape." A gang of criminals invade the Mansion. The neighbours call the Police however an anti Wire Receptionist answers but fails to report the crime.

Meanwhile.

Officer Ryan Debton tell's Mitchell "The bank robbers are in a Voodoo cult. They say a well known Voodoo Doctor has the ability to create hallucinations. Mitchell laughs at the thought of Voodoo. He says "I'm a Man of Science. There's no respected evidence that suggests Voodoo is possible."

Panic Room.

Janice and Cyril watch as the burglar steel everything of value. A Man ties Janice and Cyril up. The Voodoo Doctor has a Jamaican accent. He tell's Janice "Your Husband get's involved in business that don't concern him. He brought this on your Family." The Voodoo Doctor throws a hand full of bones onto the Living room table, He then starts to prey. Lots of insects walk and fly into the Living room. They crawl over Janice and Cyril. The Voodoo Doctor has 3 Voodoo dolls. He stabs Janice's Voodoo doll several times. He finally stabs Janice's Voodoo doll in the heart. Janice dies.

Officer Debton suggests Mitchell is being hunted by the criminal underground. "The Policeman say's "You put them out of business. The Establishment are recruiting anyone who potentially has a problem with you. Your in the middle of a war."

Hallucination.

Janice is obviously only hallucinating. Her and Cyril are in the panic room. However the house is set on fire.

Meanwhile.

Mitchell tries to phone Janice and Cyril but the Voodoo Doctor has their phones. Janice left it on the livingroom table. He tries to send a text message. When Janice does'nt answer he assumes the worse. A Police Officer tells Officer Debton there's a fire at Mitchells house. Both Mitchell and Officer Debton assume the worse especially once the teleporter device doesn't work.

Firemen.

The masked criminals try to prevent the firemen from putting out the house fire. Janice and Cyril are forced to leave the panic room. Several other houses are set on fire. Meanwhile Mitchell's neighbours try to rescue Janice and Cyril. The Voodoo Doctor is still there too. He has a Mitchell doll. He stabs it with a needle. Mitchell screams in pain. Officer Ryan Debton ask him if he's ok? Mitchell say's "I don't no".

The criminals run as soon as the Police arrive. Several are shot with the (e) musket. The atmosphere is calm until the Voodoo Doctor walks out of the burning house into the front garden. He throws his needle to the floor then he throws Janice's Voodoo doll into the burning flames, Fortunately it's caught by Cyril.

The situation is far from over. Janice tries to run away but the Voodoo Doctor manages to hold Cyril as a Hostage. Mitchell tries to offer himself instead. He walks towards the Voodoo Doctor with his hands up. From no where Kronos the dog bites the Voodoo Doctor. Misses Fox's pet dog Pep attacks him too. The Police take the opportunity to arrest the Voodoo Doctor.

News.

Mitchell is looking at his ex Wife Beth's photo. One second she's not in it then all of all sudden she runs into shot. She smiles at the camera. By the end of the week all old photographs return to normal. The Voodoo doctor is in jail. He takes up arts and craft. He makes a Mitchell Doll.

Primetime.

All traces of time travel are blocked. All other dimensions will need to invent time travel on their own.

The End.

THE WIRE – 5

BILLIONAIRE MITCHELL ARMSTRONG IS HUNTED BY THE CRIMINAL UNDERGROUND. MEANWHILE A STRANGE SHIFT IN THE SPACE TIME CONTINUUM RUINS ALL PHOTOGRAPHS

CHAPTER ONE

LAPSY, DAPSY AND TAPSY

Proffessor David Clayton's 4 year relationship, With his wife Claire is going through a bad patch. His Wife is sat on the single sofa. She use to sit on the large sofa next to him. Instead of David she is stroking the Cats. He can't believe that he is jealous of his own pets. That was 6 years ago.

Press Conference. The Present Day.

The first compulsory school for Dogs is opened. It's the year 3019. Obviously the Dogs aren't taught the 3 R's. Instead the school teacher's train and examine the 4 legged students until graduation. Successful Dog's are employed in various roles. Exceptional Dogs may achieve positions such as guide Dogs, Police Dogs and sheep Dogs. There is a concern that the Family not the pet resives the wages for the Dogs hard work.

Clarke is Back.

There has been many recorded attacks on Clarke's Clones. He decides to fight back after his number 2 is murdered. Many believe Clarke's super Human Clones will take over Man as the dominant species on Earth. However Rule Price has even given the Police free mobile teleporters.

P.C Lee Neilson is criticised for his failure to capture Rule aka Clarke. P.C Lee Neilson responds to his criticism by saying. "You may not agree with what I've done so far but I garrentee you'll call the Police when you need us."

News.

There's a Terrorist attack on Windsor Castle. P.C Lee Neilson hires more Police officers.

The Wire - Reality Program - Real Crimes,

The Police Officer is undercover and he wears the state of the art Wire. The first official episode of the Wire involved a Scottish drug dealer who's also a suspected Cop killer. P.C Smith survived the Wire. The drug lord was brought to justice. However instead of simply getting a trusted member of the community to go undercover the Police only used other officers. All they could do is hope no one recognises them.

1 Police Officer didn't survive the first series. He was murdered by a serial killer. He was killed soon as the serial killer discovered he was a Police Officer. The reality program had to be cancelled or it had to evolve. 2 years ago the Goverment introduced the 1st Compulsory community Police Service. This meant any British citizen could and would be expected to enlist as a Police Officer when called up.

The Devils Alter.

Mitchell is informed that people are traveling back in time inorder to commit the most serious of crimes imaginable. Players take part in this new sport do so knowing that the crimes will not register in this dimension.

1.pm. Mitchell receives a phone call from the Police department. They ask him to be a undercover Policeman. Mitchell insists he is too famous to go undercover. He's 1 of the most recognised Men in the World. He's as recognisable as Einstein. However the neural network has been redesigned. This new tech will help Mitchell to go undercover.

The Neural Network - 3000.

It already could recognise and identify various different animals from one another. However It's facial recognition can even work in reverse. The neural network can change the eye of the beholder. Mitchell is doughtful until the machine is turned off, His son Cyril was in the office all along. Mitchell didn't even recognise his own Son.

More Tests.

Doctor Olan upgraded the technology to allow spy's to fool A.I Technology not just the Human mind. Doc Olan has 2 pictures 1 is of Mitchell's Wife, Janice the other is of Mitchell's ex wife. Doc Olan ask's Mitchell to point at the picture of his current Wife. Mitchell incorrectly selects his ex Wife's picture. The other images involved animals, Celebrities, And other random objects. Mitchell fails the exam by 100%.

News - Little Armstrong. Aka The Hero Dog.

Proffessor Mitchell Armstrong's pet Dog saves Mitchell's Son Cyril from his next door neighbours Alsatian Dog. Kronos is only 3 years old. Here are picture of him resiving an award for bravery yesterday. Kronos also saved Mitchell and Janice's life from the Voodoo Doctor.

The Lock Ness Monster Hunters. - Mobile Teleporter.

Mitchell activates the Wire as soon as he resives a call. He meets a Man called Thomas Wolf. He gives Mitchell an envelope. It has a name and 3 photographs. Mitchell travels back in time within an hour. His investigation leads him to lock ness. It's a time when the lock ness monster still existed. Mitchell actually see's the lock ness monster with his own 2 eyes. However within a minute of being there it's killed by hunters from the future. Using simple harpoons. Fortunately other simular creators escaped. Did any stay behind?

Mitchells discovers that hunters are going back in time to kill famous people. Mitchell's mark is called Jane Hallon. He can do what ever he wants to do. Rape her or even kill her. Mitchell is still wearing a Wire. He turns it off. He finds and tells Jane the situation. The next day Mitchell tells Richard Traine about hunting. Thomas Wolf is arrested the next time the 2 Men meet. If found guilty he'll be expected to face 30 years in jail. Mitchell's surprised when Thomas is found not guilty.

Janice vs Mitchell - Mitchell vs The Police.

Janice insists that Mitchell confronts the Police about the release of Thomas Wolf. He tells her "I'm not above the law." He still tries to use his influence to get Thomas Wolf re-arrested. The Goverment concedes that they can not Police the infinity of alternate dimension. It's simular to the War on drugs, It simply can not be won without an amendment on freedom. Mitchell investigates further. He discovers 4 Judges have been recently been murdered. The Police insist this has no connection to why Thomas Wolf was released.

The Police.

Footballer Ian Meed was murdered earlier this morning. We are not allowed to travel back in time to save his life. Not even to find out who the murderer is.

Proffessor David Clayton - Interview.

"There are questions, Therefore there are answers. Vast numbers of the poor majority are extremely clever. There's an Italian stallion within all of us, All we need is an Apollo Creed. That's all I needed. I had studied politics at university but I had no intention of affiliating myself with any of the major parties.

Mitchell receives the call. He hasn't got the Wire or his neural network. They meet in an abandoned warehouse. Gavin Noir hands Mitchell an envelope. His mark is a wealthy Irish Man called Jack O'Rielly. He has connections with the old I.R.A. He has committed murders in the past. Remember the murder victims in this dimension will still be alive when you return to your own dimension. Mitchell wants to choose his own mark but Gavin say's "That's not how it works."

The Raid.

It's 8:30 pm. The Police raid the warehouse. Mitchell is arrested. The Police have resived an anonymous tip. There is evidence that people have been traveling to parallel dimensions, Simply to kill. We can confirm the Establishment has resived payment to organise the murders. Mitchell has been set up.

Mitchell Escapes - The Ultimate Power.

Thomas Wolf saves Mitchell. He uses a mobile teleporter. He pretended to use Mitchell as a Human shield. The Police were caught off guard. They did'nt put up much of a resistance. Thomas tells Mitchell that he's an undercover Police Officer too. He tell's Mitchell that he's been investigating the serial killer who's been murdering Judges. Gavin Noir is arrested. The Police say Mitchell no longer works with them and he hasn't been for a week.

Thomas Wolf say's "Police always had the licence to kill but the ultimate Power is having the right to get away with plain old murder. It was the Police invented the Bond experience/Holiday. There's only a thin blue line between criminals and the law. The only difference is criminals can't arrest Police Officers."

Entrapment.

Thomas say's "They was going to kill you. I've heard about M.I.5 agents who have assassinate the president of America as an induction. They become part of the Establishment. Some are members of Mitchell's board others are from other companies e.g Politiions, And terrorist groups.

Resurface - Closed.

Mitchell is in the future. He's been in hiding for a while. Thomas Wolf buys all of Mitchell's shopping. The future that Mitchell has travelled into does'nt have very many Police Stations. Teleportation meant there was no need for more than 1 per city. Where there was bus stops or train stops,

Now there are teleportation pods. Mitchell is still a fugitive and the neural network no longer protects him.

Add - Execution.

The future head of Police is still Lee Neilson. He informs the last remaining Police Officers that the hunt for Mitchell Armstrong is considered as a main priority. Mitchell is being hunted by Bounty Hunters too. He's head is worth £500,000. The Police get 50% of the reward.

Search Warrent.

This means the Police can legally teleport into any property at any time when in search of criminals at large. It's 11 pm. Facts show that black houses are searched more than white houses. A Bounty Hunter teleports into Mitchell's living room. However Thomas Wolf predicted this. That's why Mitchell was sleeping in the kitchen. He's woken by the noise of the Bounty Hunter. He packs up his sleeping bag and escapes through the back garden.

Mitchell is on the open streets. He was the 1st Man to travel into the future even if it was a mistake. Future time travel was mastered a while ago. Mitchell is walking on Tenton street. He's wearing a cap but a stranger still recognises him. Lots of others recognise him too. Everyone steers at him. They ask him if he's on an adventure to save the World. His face appears on the large electric billboard. Several people appear on TV for a brief moment. However Mitchell's face is on there for an hour.

Collision Risk - 70%

The Bounty Hunter arrives at Night City. He use's his teleporter app. He thinks he seen Mitchell. He walks over to him. All of a sudden Mitchell is saved by Janice and his now 17 year old son Cyril. Cyril types away on his laptop. Suddenly the neural network makes everyone in the city centre look just like Mitchell. Male and Female. The Bounty Hunter's can't tell which is the real Mitchell Armstrong. Even they look like him but not the Police. Mitchell ask's if he and Janice are still together? She say's "I can't tell you". She gives Mitchell a mobile teleporter. The electronic billboard has a picture of Lee Neilson. Mitchell travels back to his original time. He heads straight to Lee Neilson's office.

Fail Safe 2 - The Monopoly Of Protection.

Thomas Wolf is already there. He understands how and why Lee did what he did. Mitchell say's the 1 word is obsoletion. So you and other Police Officers simply aim to keep your selves in employment. We are all on the verge of the litteral extinction of crime. You also wanted to ensure you maintained a monopoly of protection. Killing conscripted Police Officers will achives that.

Thomas say's "I am officer Thomas Wolf and I am the law. The church still insists that suicide is a mortal sin however many followers of God disagree. To many it is salvation. What if the Devil and his followers have a guilty conscience. Then suicide is the only salvation that translates to i'm sorry. He orders Lee Neilson to commit suicide. He hands him a pill. He promises it will be painless. Lee Neilson swallows the pill and dies. Thomas say's "It was a Police Officer who killed Ian Meed."

Mitchell vs Janice. Later That Night.

Janice say's the facts are that victims of crime need help. Mitchell say's the public can protect themselves. The law is restricting self defence. The organised concept of Police is now owned by Police. They still have a Monopoly on protection. Can they be trusted? Janice say's "The emergency services are here to help. Mitchell say's "I know." We do not need to ask the Police to protect. We don't need to ask Firemen either. I understand that they and we are only Human.

Time Management. Overkill.

The Goverment officially abandon conscription community Police force and the Wire reality programme. Early stages of what Mitchell saw in the future has started to happen.

Mitchell, Janice and Clake watching TV. Clarke say's This cartoon isn't just fiction, it's based on reality. Talking dog's and cats." Clake takes Mitchell and Janice into the future. There are no humans. Only talking, inteligent animals. He say's We have to stop dogs for schools. These cartoons are a warning.".....all of them.

Mitchell puts the radio on.

If she advertised it
I wud buy it.

If she advertised it
I wud buy it.

If she advertised it
I wud buy it.

Yo I only bought it.
Bca she endorced it.

C.

She wears her cute smile. Rap
As a fashion item. Sung
She cn even wears - being in love. Rap.
She wears being naked Rap
As a fashion item. Sung
N sexy as type of make up. X2.

V1.

I meet at her at a pajama party.
I did'nt knw her - Bt she knw of me.

She stood out of the crowd.
I did'nt try 2 pull her bcz i ws bound - 2 get turned down.

She ws perfection - No illusion.
I shudda known she ws a stripper - frm male intuition.

She sharp 2 - Always on the clock.
Bt she Definately a stripper - I cud tell that frm a –- mile off.

Everything she did ws flurtious.

PAUSE.

Bt is she's only pretendin 2 b premicuios?

PAUSE.

She reluctant 2 tell me wot she DOES 2 bring home the bacon.
– As if she thought i ws a Vegitarian.

C.

She wears her cute smile. Sung
As a fashion item. Rap
She cn even wears - being in love. Sung.
She wears being naked.
As a fashion item. Sung
N sexy as type of make up. X2.

V2.

Sometimes she's dresses 2 slutty
N her personality way 2 bubbly.
At 1st i ws scared 2 take 2 the pub with me.

Other girls r quick 2 ask there men if he's been with her.
Meaning in her. Bt his nt her heart, kidneys or liver.

He's bound 2 say no - Even if he did.
N act like he nt in the least bit intrested.

In my horney little devil.
Who only told me wot she did 4 livin ONCE WE TOOK things the next
level.

Yeah – We condom got it on
Bca we both knw mom rhymes with come

1 on 1
By then my friend had already told me he recognised her n where frm.

I weren't surprised - She 1 of those women.
That mek u say yo!!! Wot do u think she does 4 a livin.

The mind - boggles.
She so hot - I cud finally tek off my bear goggles.

Nw no matter wot it is - if she in or on it.
U cn assume i own 2 or 3 copies.

Even if i dn't need it or want it.
I'll probably end buyin – 2 many of it.

C.

She wears her cute smile. Sung
As a fashion item. Rap
She cn even wears - being in love. Sung.
She wears being naked.
As a fashion item. Sung
N sexy as type of make up. X2.

B.

Intro.

If she advertised it
I wud buy it.

If she advertised it
I wud buy it.

If she advertised it
I wud buy it.

Yo I only bought it.
Bca she endorsed it.

V3.

1ˢᵗ time i saw her at work - It almost broke my heart.
I walked in n saw her topless dancin on the bar.

In a sexy cop outfit.
lookin like the kinda girl who gets married jus 4 the weddin gifts.

Other men's eyes where almost popin out there socket. Bt it's 2 late.
Sorry man – That's my date.

She's the 1ˢᵗ stripper girl friend i've eva had.
All her friends knew that she wouldn't b my last.

It's as hard 4 them 2 quit once they've started..
ALL THE money the attention that surrounds it.

I watched her work that pole in like like she ws made 4 it.
I worked in factory man - Nobody shud b paid 4 this.

She makes me rise. Reminds me of helium ballons.
She the type of girl who's sometimes slept with more than 1 bloke - in a room.

Whooo! —-PAUSE.

She cud win the lotto.
N she wud still want 2 work scene n work that pole.

Sumtimes she goes out - with no panties no bra.
She nt a hooker - no - She did'nt want 2 go –- that far.

So as long as u got a cash card u wnt need –-no car.
Strippin in her blood nw 2 get her off it UR gonna need a vampire.

C.

She wears her cute smile. Sung
As a fashion item. Rap
She cn even wears - being in love. Sung.
She wears being naked. Rap
As a fashion item. Sung
N sexy as type of make up. X2. Rap

B. Then repeat c.

The End.